In the Garden

Written by Margo Gates

Illustrated by Lisa Hunt

GRL Consultants, Diane Craig and Monica Marx, Certified Literacy Specialists

Lerner Publications ◆ Minneapolis

Note from a GRL Consultant
This Pull Ahead leveled book has been carefully designed for beginning readers.
A team of guided reading literacy experts has reviewed and leveled the book to
ensure readers pull ahead and experience success.

Lerner Publications Company
A division of Lerner Publishing Group, Inc.
241 First Avenue North
Minneapolis, MN 55401 USA

For reading levels and more information, look up this title at www.lernerbooks.com.

Main body text set in Mikado 24/41
Typeface provided by Hannes von Doehren.

Photo Acknowledgments
The images in this book are used with the permission of: Lisa Hunt

Library of Congress Cataloging-in-Publication Data

Names: Gates, Margo, author. | Hunt, Lisa (Lisa Jane), 1973– illustrator.
Title: In the garden / by Margo Gates ; illustrated by Lisa Hunt.
Description: Minneapolis : Lerner Publications, [2020] | Series: Science all around me
    (Pull ahead readers-Fiction) | Includes index.
Identifiers: LCCN 2018056970 (print) | LCCN 2018057624 (ebook) | ISBN 9781541562325
    (eb pdf) | ISBN 9781541558540 (lb : alk. paper) | ISBN 9781541573376 (pb : alk. paper)
Subjects: LCSH: Readers (Primary) | Gardens—Juvenile fiction.
Classification: LCC PE1119 (ebook) | LCC PE1119 .G38445 2020 (print) | DDC 428.6/2—dc23

LC record available at https://lccn.loc.gov/2018056970

Manufactured in the United States of America
2-51161-46235-6/9/2021

Contents

In the Garden

George looks at his garden.
He sees dirt in his garden.

George sees flowers
in his garden.
"The flowers grow,"
said George.

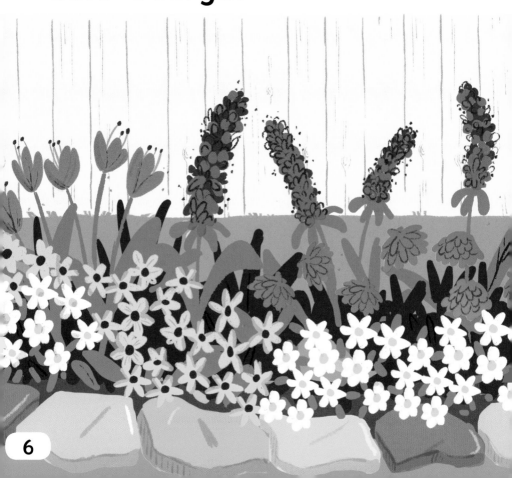

George sees rocks
in his garden.

George sees bugs
in his garden.
"The bugs crawl,"
said George.

George sees bees
in his garden.
"The bees buzz,"
said George.

"I like my garden,"
said George.

Did You See It?

bees

bugs

dirt

flowers

garden

rocks

Index